D0585549

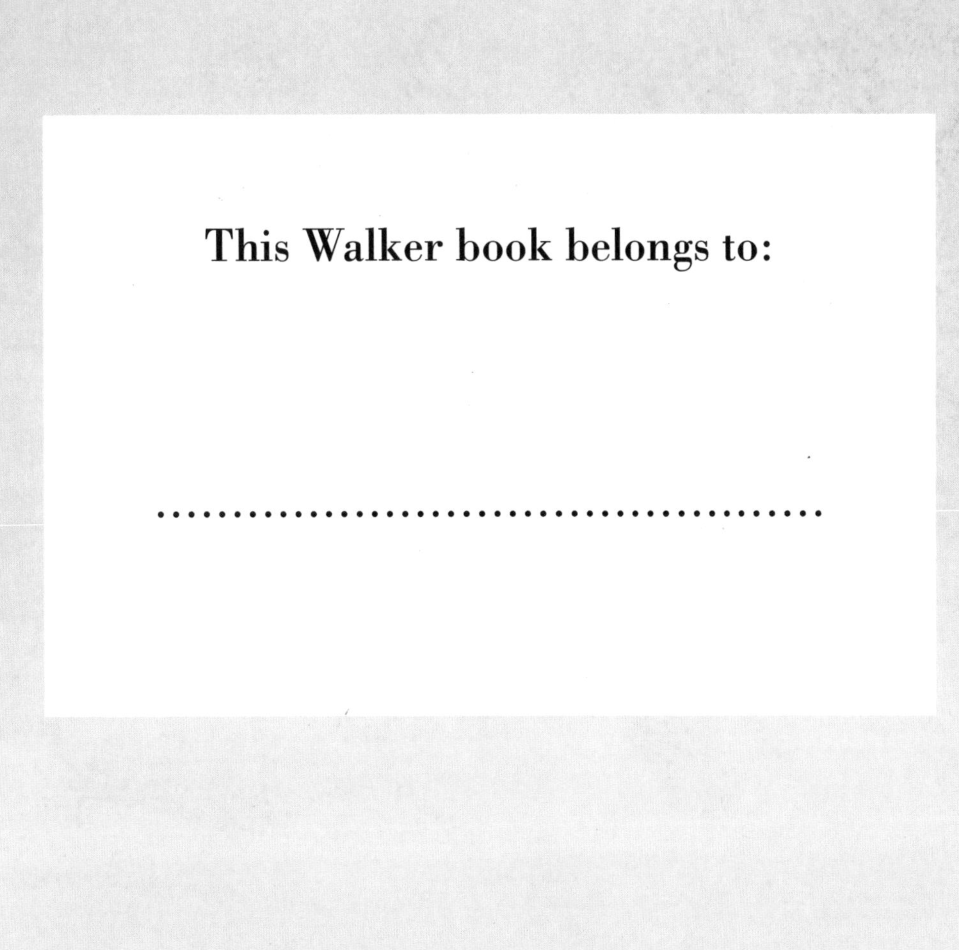

This Walker book belongs to:

....

For Theseus – I.B.
To Petr, with thanks – R.J.

First published 2021 by Walker Books Ltd, 87 Vauxhall Walk, London SE11 5HJ

2 4 6 8 10 9 7 5 3 1

This book has been typeset in Bodoni

Printed in China

British Library Cataloguing in Publication Data: a catalogue record for this book is available from the British Library

ISBN 978-1-4063-8942-5

www.walker.co.uk

The Seed of Doubt

IRENA BRIGNULL *Illustrated by* RICHARD JONES

In fields, flat and wide, lived a young boy and his father.
After school, the boy would help his father on the farm,
tending to the crops and the animals.

The boy loved the farm – the meadows and the brook, the barn and the hen-house. But he dreamed of a world beyond.

A world where mountain ranges rose sharp through clouds,

where oceans swelled with hidden depths,

where cities stretched with skyscrapers.

A world where he could do anything and be anyone.

Every evening before bed, the boy would tell his father of his dreams.
"When I am bigger, I'm going to climb up high. I'm going to climb the tallest tree in the largest forest, then the highest peak of all the mountains, and then ..." the boy paused as he looked out at the night sky, "then I'm going to fly right up to the moon."

His father would listen and nod, put his
arm around his son and kiss his head.
"You know you can do anything," he would
always say, "as long as you believe it."

The next day, the boy was walking through the fields when a bird, swift and sleek, flew overhead. As the bird passed him, it called out and something fell from its beak.

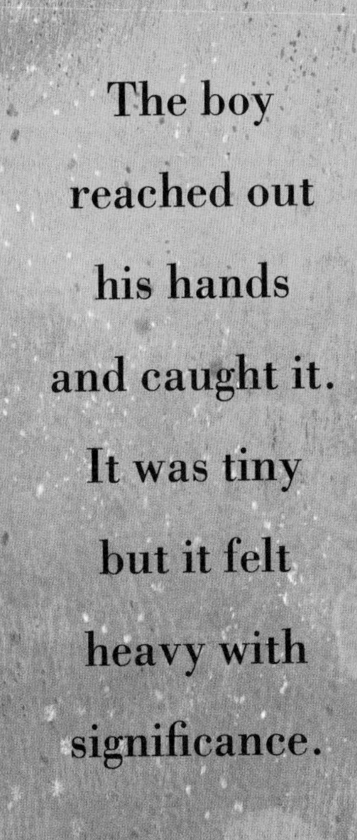

The boy
reached out
his hands
and caught it.
It was tiny
but it felt
heavy with
significance.

It was a seed.

The boy dug a hole
and in it he planted
the seed.

When he covered it up,
it was as though it
had never existed.

A few weeks later,
a sprout of green
appeared.

And before long,
the sprout became
a shoot …

and the shoot
became
a sapling.

The tree grew so impossibly
fast and impossibly tall that
no one could believe it.

At first, the tree was like a wish come true

and the boy couldn't wait until he

was big enough to climb it.

But as the seasons passed and the boy grew bigger,

his dreams got smaller.

Instead of thinking of all that he could do,

he thought more of
what he could not.

Now when he saw the tree,
he felt more fear than joy.
He still longed to climb it but
he doubted that he was strong
enough, or brave enough,
or sure enough.

In the evenings, instead of telling his father of his dreams, he spoke about how the hens were laying and the cows were milking.

And when he looked out at the night sky, the top of the tree seemed to touch the stars and the moon seemed so very far away.

One day, the father saw the boy
standing in the tree's great shadow and
he stopped to lay a hand upon his shoulder.
"Doubt," he said softly, "is like a seed.
It starts off tiny but it sure grows fast."

The boy looked up at the tree's branches
that reached so high into the sky. His
forehead furrowed like the fields after
ploughing. His eyes misted over, tears
falling from them like rain.

"What do I do?"

he whispered.

His father wiped the tears from his son's cheeks. "Remember what I've always told you? You can do anything … anything you want…"

"As long as I believe it," the boy finished.

The boy reached out a hand and felt the tree's rough bark beneath his fingers. As he looked up, he saw a squirrel, clever and curious, peering down at him.
Up scampered the squirrel and up the boy followed.

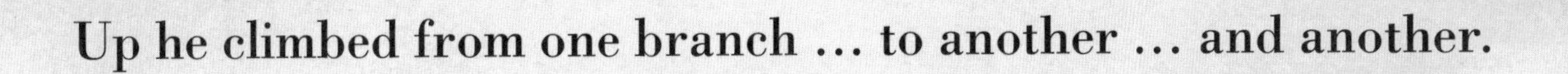
Up he climbed from one branch … to another … and another.

His father watched as he rose higher.

"*That's it*," he said to himself.

"*That's it*," he said

under his breath.

Soon he felt tired. He wanted to stop and rest but he knew he must keep going.

Up and up, the boy went, passing the squirrels and the birds on his way.

"*Keep going*," his father murmured.

When the boy looked down, he'd never felt so scared. His body started shaking, his head spinning. He wanted to climb down, to go home, to never see the tree again. But he knew he mustn't give up.

"Don't give up!" his father called to him.

So the boy kept on climbing and believing …

believing and climbing … higher …

and higher … and higher …

until there it was.

The top of the tree.

“What do you see?” came his father’s voice, loud and strong from far below.

The boy lifted his head and his spirits lifted with it.

As he looked out, he could see far and wide across the plains.

And beyond them, he could see his dreams.

He could see snow-capped mountain ranges and deep blue oceans and vast cities all laid out before him, ready to explore.

"Everything," the boy cried out to the sky, to his father, to himself. "I can see *everything*."

His father laughed and wept with pride.
And the boy – he felt on top of the world.

He felt like he could do anything and go anywhere.

He could even fly to the moon if he believed it.

THE END